STRANGER DANGER

SIT, STAY, SLEEP COZY MYSTERIES
BOOK 2

PATTI BENNING

SUMMER PRESCOTT BOOKS PUBLISHING

Copyright 2025 Summer Prescott Books

All Rights Reserved. No part of this publication nor any of the information herein may be quoted from, nor reproduced, in any form, including but not limited to: printing, scanning, photocopying, or any other printed, digital, or audio formats, without prior express written consent of the copyright holder.

**This book is a work of fiction. Any similarities to persons, living or dead, places of business, or situations past or present, is completely unintentional.

CHAPTER ONE

The kennels rang with barks, howls, and the melodious baying of a hound, and the air smelled of dog and professional grade, pet-safe disinfectant. Despite the recent cleaning, a tumbleweed of dog fur floated out of one of the kennels, propelled by the force of its occupant's wagging tail.

Sadie Barton, in a set of damp, sky-blue scrubs with her arms loaded down with dog bowls, couldn't have been happier.

"Does Miss Luna need to be brushed again?" she asked in a singsong voice as she stopped in front of the husky's kennel.

The black and white northern breed was the one who was responsible for the tumbleweed of fur — and the howls. Luna's family had just moved from

Maine, to a town forty-five minutes away. To say the dog was still adjusting to the heat would be an understatement. Yesterday, Sadie had filled a kiddie pool with cool water and ice cubes to give her a chance to cool off outside; otherwise, the husky spent all day hiding inside where the air conditioning kept the worst of the heat at bay. The indoor-outdoor runs were a blessing, since they meant the dogs could choose whether they wanted to brave the Georgia summer or not.

Despite not being suited for the warm weather, Luna looked happy as she danced around inside of her kennel, waiting for Sadie to open the door. The bowl of dog food in her hand probably had something to do with it, but Sadie liked to think her hard work to make sure each of her guests was comfortable and happy was paying off.

After putting Luna's food bowl down, she moved on to the next kennel, where Rosco, the young and energetic lab mix who was their very first regular client, was bouncing straight into the air. He let out a high-pitched bark at the apex of each jump, unable to contain his excitement at the promise of food. This was his third stay at Sit, Stay, Sleep Motel and Boarding. His owner, Beth, liked to visit her daughter's family on the weekends, but they had a new baby and

Rosco was a little too rambunctious to accompany her.

He had been their very first guest, and Sadie hoped he would keep coming back for a long time. She and Penny, her best friend slash business partner, had been on the verge of giving the entire business up as a bad idea when Beth booked his first stay.

"Here you go, handsome; kibble mixed with boiled chicken bits, just like your mom makes it."

She left him to gulp down his food while she carried the last bowl to the occupant of the last kennel. While Rosco had a special place in her heart, this dog owned a bigger chunk of her heart than most people did. Unlike the other dogs, he sat politely on his bed, but the quiver in his muscles and string of drool hanging from his lips gave away his excitement for the meal.

"Hey, buddy," she said as she opened the door to the kennel. "Sorry to keep you waiting."

Unlike the other dogs, she wasn't worried he would run out. Jasper was her dog and had over a year of training under his belt. As far as she was concerned, he was the handsomest foxhound in the whole world, and one of the best dogs she had ever met.

She set his bowl down on the ground. He glanced

down at it, then stared back up at her, his soft brown eyes asking a question as clear as any she had heard from a human.

"Okay."

At that single word, he lunged forward and dove into his bowl, his white-tipped tail wagging so fast it blurred. She backed out of the kennel, re-latched the chain-link door, then raised her arms over her head to stretch her aching shoulders. It was only mid-morning, but running a boarding kennel was a lot of work, even with just three guests — well, two, since Jasper didn't count. She only had him in the kennel right now since she thought he would be more entertained there, where he could see and smell the other dogs, than he would be alone in the apartment above the motel's lobby while she helped Penny with the other part of their business.

She knew it wouldn't always be this way, but the past few weeks had been stuffed to the brim with almost nothing but marketing, cleaning, and as much DIY renovation as they could get away with. Running a boarding kennel out of the back of a motel made sense to *her* but a lot of the people she tried to advertise to were confused at first. She suspected many of them had never tried to take a road trip with a dog. Even though all but one of their motel rooms were going to be pet-friendly — she and Penny both wanted somewhere comfortable for their guests with allergies to stay — leaving a dog alone in a motel room was just asking for trouble, and leaving a dog alone in the car was a bad idea even at the best of times, but down here in Georgia, it would be deadly for most of the year.

What was a vacationer supposed to do with their beloved pet if they wanted to do something that wasn't pet-friendly? Why, board them for the day at the Sit, Stay and Sleep kennel! That was Sadie's idea, anyway. So far, all of their clients had been locals, and they had only had a few of them. She hadn't had time to start offering dog training lessons yet, but she was hoping once she did, things would pick up. Getting the motel rooms up to code and officially opening their doors to human guests would help too… if they could convince anyone to stay there with the motel's sordid history.

Sadie forced the worries from her mind as she left the kennel room and walked through the laundry room to the motel's lobby. All they could do was try their best. The few boarding clients they had gotten so far were enough to keep them afloat or at least pay for their electricity bill and the cheapest frozen burritos and ramen noodles they could buy at the grocery store. They had drained their savings accounts to pay for the motel in cash — no lender would have given them a mortgage for it with the state it had been in — which meant they didn't have a monthly mortgage payment to worry about, though their bank accounts were all but empty.

For now, Sadie was just trying not to think about the fact that their insurance and property tax payments would be due in three months. If things weren't better by then, they might have to revisit selling the motel and moving back to Lexington.

Stepping outside into the humid, overcast day, she turned left and walked down the row of motel rooms. There were ten rooms in total — and eight kennel runs out back — but for now, they were only able to use nine of them for guests. Penny was staying in Room Three until she could draw enough of a salary to rent a place in Greencreek.

Sadie felt bad that her best friend was relegated to living out of a motel room, but they both agreed it made the most sense for Sadie to live in the on-site apartment, since she needed to be on the premises in case there was an emergency with the dogs overnight.

A week ago, they had used the last of their savings to hire a company to come out and install cheap but new carpets in all ten of the motel rooms. They had already purchased all new mattresses and linens and had finished painting the rooms before they replaced the carpets. Rooms One through Six were now fully complete and ready for guests; the motel rooms would be a little basic and boring for now, but at least they would be clean and — Sadie hoped — comfortable.

They were putting the finishing touches on Room Seven today. Penny was already hard at work; she had a hammer in her hand and two nails clenched between her lips when Sadie walked in. They had picked up some cheap artwork at a thrift shop a few days ago in an effort to add a little more life to the rooms. The picture Penny was currently hanging was a print of an oil painting of a lovely, sunlit grove with a stream running through it.

"Here, let me take that," Sadie said. She supported the frame while Penny marked where the nails should go, then stepped back while her friend hammered them in.

She wouldn't insult her friend by saying it, but she was impressed. Penny's family was the sort of well-off, old money family that almost lived in a different world from most people. She wasn't sure her friend had so much as lifted a hammer for the first twenty years of her life. There had been a few bruised fingers for both of them when they started working on the motel. Sadie might have been a little more familiar around hammers and nails, but that didn't mean she was good at that sort of thing, but now they were practically pros.

She hung the picture up, the tilt to the right immediately noticeable. Well… they weren't novices anymore, at least. They still had a lot to learn.

"Dang it," Penny muttered. "Where did that level go?"

"We probably should have checked before hammering the nails in." Sadie laughed, but she pitched in to help look until she heard the sound of a car turning into the motel's parking lot. They were on Highway 78, just a couple of miles past the turn into town, and so far they'd had more people using their parking lot to turn around than actual guests, so her hopes weren't high as she peeked out through the open door. When she saw the old station wagon pull to a stop in front of the lobby door, and heard the driver's side door pop open, she felt a thrill go through her.

Another customer. Or a *potential* customer. She had to go and lock them down, quick.

"Good luck. I'll be right back," she said with a hurried wave to her friend as she raced out of the room. She wished she had taken the time to change out of her damp scrubs, but it had been days since they'd had someone drop by unexpectedly, and she had been planning to spend most of the day cleaning, which always ended up being a surprisingly dirty endeavor.

She strode down the sidewalk that led down the row of rooms toward the lobby, trying not to look as eager as she felt. Even the appearance of the man who got out of the car, who was about her height and lean, and was wearing a ratty old ball cap pulled low over his eyes, which themselves were covered by dark sunglasses despite the overcast sky, didn't dampen her enthusiasm much especially when she saw the dog that he let out of the back.

The dog was tall, with long, silky golden blonde fur that flowed like water over her lean frame, an Afghan hound. The breed was unmistakable, despite it being the first one Sadie had seen in person. She was immediately in love.

"Oh, my goodness," she crooned, forgetting that she wanted to act casual. "Who do we have here?"

She forced herself to stop a few feet away from the gorgeous dog; she looked friendly, but Sadie hated it when people tried to pet Jasper without asking first and she didn't want to be a hypocrite.

"Her name's Cleo," the man said.

He held out the dog's leash, which was made out of buttery soft leather. Sadie took it reflexively as he ducked back into the car to fetch a folded paper and an envelope. He held both out to her, then paused, looking around as if he had just noticed the cracked asphalt, the lawn that was more crabgrass than real grass, and the laminated sign that was stapled to the post by the road, rather than the lovely wooden sign Sadie wished they could afford.

"You do boarding?"

He sounded doubtful, but Luna chose that moment to let out a howl from the kennels out back. Sadie nodded. "We definitely do. Normally I'd ask for a reservation in advance, but we have space if you need to drop her off right now. Let's go into the lobby, and I'll get her checked in."

He shook his head and shoved the paper and envelope into her free hand. "It's going to be at least a week. Maybe two." He hesitated, then added, "Take care of her. She's a good dog."

"Wait—"

Before Sadie could say anything else, he got back into the driver's seat and slammed the door shut. She had to back away with Cleo to be sure he wouldn't hit them as he backed out. After putting the car into drive, he peeled out of the parking lot with enough acceleration to leave tire marks on the asphalt.

Sadie stared after him, then looked down at the dog whose leash she was still gripping. Cleo looked back up at her with dark eyes, then pointed her long muzzle down the road where the station wagon had disappeared and let out a worried whine.

CHAPTER TWO

Penny poked her head out of the door a few rooms down. "Everything all right?" she called out. "I heard tires screech."

"I'm not sure," Sadie said. "Some guy just dropped his dog off, without even leaving his name."

"Weird." Her friend approached and held a hand out. Cleo sniffed it politely, then sat down and turned her head to look down the road again. "Does she seem all right?"

Sadie looked down at the dog. She looked healthy and well-groomed, and she didn't see any obvious injuries. She knew the asphalt had to be hot on her paws, though, even with how overcast it was.

"I think so. He gave me these papers too. We can

look everything over and decide what to do from there."

As soon as she started moving, Cleo fell into a perfect heel at her side. Penny opened the door to the lobby to let them through. The air conditioning wrapped around the three of them like a cool blanket.

"Can you fill up one of the dog bowls with water for her?" Sadie asked. "I don't want to take her into the kennel room yet. Not until I know whether she's up to date on her vaccines and get a chance to look her over."

The last thing she needed was to send one of her canine guests home with fleas or kennel cough. Cleo looked healthy, but it wouldn't be fair to the other dogs' owners to demand vaccine records from them, only to expose their dogs to a dog whose medical history she didn't know.

"Yeah. I'll be right back."

While Penny went to get the water, Sadie sat in one of their uncomfortable chairs and patted her leg, hoping to encourage Cleo to approach her. The dog was staring at the door, as if hoping her owner would walk through at any second but turned toward her at the sound. She sniffed Sadie's hands and pants delicately, then rested her narrow chin on Sadie's knee. Sadie ran a hand through the silky fur on her head.

"You're gorgeous," she murmured. "And such a polite dog, too. You put Jasper to shame."

She wanted nothing more than to spend the next hour petting the dog, but she needed to get to the bottom of this first, so she opened the envelope. It was stuffed full of cash. She flipped through the bills quickly to make sure he hadn't hidden a note between them. It was nice that he hadn't dropped Cleo off without paying, but at the moment she was more concerned with the dog's welfare than money.

After setting the envelope of cash down on the seat next to her, she unfolded the piece of paper. It was a photocopy of Cleo's vet records — the dog's full name was Cleopatra, and according to the records, she was three years old and spayed and was up to date on everything Sadie required and more. That was a relief, but the relief was short-lived when she realized that all of the owner's identifying information had been blacked out. Even the vet clinic's name had been redacted. She felt like she was reading a classified government document, not a dog's vaccine records.

"Did he leave a note?" Penny asked as she came back into the room. She set the bowl of water down next to Cleo, who took a few grateful laps from it.

"No, just some cash and her vet records," Sadie

said. She held the paper out to her friend. "He hid all of the owner's information, and there's no way to figure out which vet clinic she was taken to, either."

Penny took the paper with a frown. "'The owner'? You think the guy who dropped her off *isn't* the owner?"

"I don't know. The whole thing was weird. He didn't give me his name or any contact information; all he told me was her name, and that she would need to be here for a week or two."

Penny set the paper down and picked the envelope up to begin counting the cash. "What do you think?" she asked as she flipped rapidly through the bills.

"I don't know." Sadie looked down at the dog, who was sniffing her shoes. "I think… it's possible she was stolen."

The thought made her feel sick, but it was the only thing that made sense. What other explanation could there be for the secrecy, otherwise? She had no idea why someone would send a recently stolen dog to a boarding kennel, but she could hardly even fathom the thought of stealing someone's obviously loved and cared for dog in the first place.

"That would be bad," Penny said. "The last thing we need is to get caught up in a dog theft ring. Should we call the police?"

"Maybe," Sadie said. "At least to ask if there are any reports of missing Afghan hounds that match her description."

"I'll call the sheriff's department," Penny decided. "What should we do with her in the meantime?"

"Well, she's up to date on everything we require," Sadie said. "I'll get her settled into one of the empty kennels for now. How much did he pay us?"

"Five-hundred dollars," Penny said. She sounded impressed. "We should probably keep the bills separate, in case they were stolen too, but at least he's an honest criminal, if he is a criminal."

While Penny handled calling the sheriff's department, Sadie brought Cleo and her water bowl back into the kennel room, where Luna and Rosco met them at their kennel gates with a cacophony of sound. Jasper watched from his kennel at the end, curious but too used to this sort of environment to be particularly bothered by a new addition. He had been in the shelter for months before she adopted him and had gone to work every day with her at her old dog training job before they moved here, so he had seen it all.

She decided to put Cleo in the first kennel, the furthest one from the other dogs. While Cleo's vet records seemed to be in order, she was still uncomfortable about how little she knew about her. The dog seemed a little nervous as Sadie opened the kennel door but entered the kennel willingly. Sadie reached down to unbuckle the dog's collar — a safety precaution, so they couldn't get hung up on anything while they were alone in their kennels — then shut the kennel door. Cleo began to explore the space immediately, which told Sadie she wasn't too nervous.

Cleo's collar was made out of gorgeous burgundy rolled leather that matched her leash, but it didn't have any tags or nameplates on it. Sadie hung it on the hook next to the kennel, then ducked into the laundry room — which doubled as storage — to fetch a bed and some treats for Cleo so she didn't have to lay on the hard floor with nothing to do. Both Luna and Rosco had supplies from home, but Sadie had stocked up on a few extras in case one of the dogs needed a change of bedding, or an owner forgot their supplies.

After setting up Cleo's dog bed, she showed the dog how the rubber, weather-resistant doggy door worked so Cleo could go outside and back in as she pleased. She briefly checked on the other dogs, collected their empty food bowls, and left Jasper with a kiss on the nose before returning to the lobby.

Penny was sitting behind the desk, in front of her

laptop when Sadie came out. She looked up and shook her head. "I talked to someone at the sheriff's department, but no one has reported a missing dog recently. They said they would make a note of it in case someone calls in. I'm trying to look online now, to see if anyone has posted her."

Sadie dragged a chair over so she could sit next to Penny as she logged onto her social media account. They had both already joined the local Greencreek group, and that was the first place Penny checked. They searched for "missing dog," "Afghan hound," and even Cleo's name, but other than a few old posts about missing pets that didn't match the dog's description, nothing came up.

"I know a few other websites for missing pets," Sadie said. "Let me try."

Penny passed the computer over to her and Sadie navigated to the website they recommended at her old training job. She plugged in Cleo's information, but nothing came up, and the dog hadn't been reported missing on any of the other websites she tried either.

"What now?" Penny asked. "Do we just hold her for that guy and try to get more information when he comes back?"

"Maybe." Sadie bit her lip. It was possible she was overreacting. Maybe the mysterious man really was Cleo's owner, and he was just a strange person who didn't realize it wasn't normal to drop his dog off at a boarding facility after exchanging no more than five words with the owner and not making a reservation. "The only other thing I can think of is to scan her for a microchip."

"Would the vet do it?"

Sadie nodded. "Yeah, or I think so, at least. Most of them do it for free. We could bring her in tomorrow."

"Do you think they might recognize her?" Penny asked. "It's a small town. There aren't very many options for veterinarians in the area."

"They might. That's a good idea, actually. We should call and see if anyone has reported her missing to them."

"We should ask, but if we take her there, everyone's going to know we have her," Penny said. She looked uncertain. "If that dog really is caught up in something bad somehow, then that means we're caught up in it too, and if anyone finds out, news will spread around town faster than we can stop it. This place already has a bad enough reputation."

Sadie leaned back in her chair, fiddling with the notepad they kept on the desk. "You're not wrong," she said at last. "But I still think scanning her for a microchip is a good idea. I won't feel right giving her back to that guy if we don't try everything we can think of first."

"Maybe we could take her to a vet in another town?" Penny suggested.

"Hold on, let me check something." Sadie pulled the computer toward herself again and navigated to her favorite online shopping website. She typed into the search bar, then scrolled through the results. "I can order my own microchip scanner online for about thirty bucks. It would get here tomorrow. It might be a good thing to have anyway. This probably won't be the only time we're concerned about a dog being stolen or lost."

"Order it," Penny said. "I'll call the vet and ask if any dogs have been reported missing lately."

Her friend looked determined — determined not to let their business get dragged down due to its proximity to a crime. Sadie knew she cared about Cleo's welfare too, but the dog was safe and sound for now. Their business, on the other hand, was already on life support.

By the time Sadie finished ordering the scanner, Penny had gotten off the phone with the vet, who hadn't been any help. Sadie couldn't believe that someone who owned a dog like Cleo, expensive, purebred, and well cared for, wouldn't be looking for her, and she didn't know whether the fact that they couldn't find any proof that she was stolen or missing was a good sign, or a bad one.

For now, she would just have to focus on making sure Cleo was happy and comfortable. Whoever really owned the dog, she knew they would be grateful to know their companion had gotten the best care possible while she was at Sit, Stay, Sleep Motel and Boarding.

CHAPTER THREE

There wasn't much more they could do about Cleo, so after a short break during which Sadie checked on the dogs, they returned to working on Room Seven. They wanted to open the motel to guests within the next two weeks, but in order to do so, they would need to pass a health and safety inspection first. She was more nervous about the upcoming inspection than she had been for the kennel inspection. She knew her way around a kennel, but they were relying on Penny's expertise for the human side of things.

She spent the day alternating between helping Penny with the handiwork and caring for the dogs. Each of them got a long walk through the woods behind the motel. They owned ten acres, and Sadie had barely had the time to explore any of it yet. The trees and undergrowth were dense, but she had discovered a series of game trails that more or less led in a loop through the back portion of the property.

The dogs each enjoyed their outings, though in different ways. Rosco was obsessed with sticks and spent the entire walk dragging progressively larger sticks behind him until he finally lost interest completely when he spotted a muddy puddle at the bottom of a hill. She managed to keep him from rolling in it, but it was a close call, and Luna's energized pulling was almost a relief in comparison. At least she wasn't constantly darting off into the bushes looking for trouble — she picked a direction and went for it.

Cleo had the best leash manners of the three and stayed glued to Sadie's side for most of the walk… which was probably a good thing, because her long, silky coat was sure to pick up leaves and burrs like no one's business. She took Jasper out last, but his walk was the longest and unlike the others, she let him be off leash for most of it. After a year of training, he had a reliable recall, though she still kept a close eye on him. No matter how well-trained he was, he was still a hound, and his nose would always be at risk of overcoming his common sense.

She was on her way back to the motel from the

game paths, Jasper trotting beside her with his tongue lolling out of his mouth, when she saw a familiar figure leaning against the kennel's back door. Sam Walker, the tenant they hadn't been expecting, but whom Sadie was glad she had met. Where she and Penny were newbies when it came to DIY and handiwork, Sam was a pro. Literally. He did lawncare for a living and did odd jobs on the side. He had been invaluable when it came to getting the kennels up and running, and though they couldn't afford to pay him for more work right now, he had insisted on lending them an old mower for free so they could at least keep the grass in front of the motel presentable.

Mowing the grass in the Georgia heat and humidity was an act of self-punishment, but she was still grateful for it. She and Penny might have been a hair impulsive when they dropped everything and moved from Lexington to open the motel, and they were going to be just scraping by for a while yet.

She raised her hand in a wave to Sam as she approached. Jasper left her side to lope over to Sam, who crouched to ruffle the dog's ears. Jasper was the sort of dog who had never met a stranger; he loved everyone, but he seemed to like Sam even more than most.

Sam straightened up and made a hand gesture,

like he was scooping something out of the air. Jasper sat, his tail whipping back and forth happily in the grass as Sam rewarded him with a pat on the shoulder. Sadie smiled at the sight; Sam was mute, and she had spent a few days working on hand gestures with Jasper so he could communicate with the dog, too. It had seemed like a fun project and a good way to practice her dog training skills on something she didn't normally do, but Sam had seemed even more touched by the gesture than she expected. She suspected he liked Jasper just as much as the foxhound liked him.

"Hey," she said, approaching to lean one shoulder against the brick wall. "What're you up to?"

He abandoned petting Jasper to take a small notepad out of his pocket; he knew sign language, but she didn't, and she imagined most people around Greencreek didn't either, so writing was the easiest way for him to communicate. She would like to learn some sign language, but she and Penny had been so busy with getting the motel up and running that her brain was too fried to absorb anything new. She would do it eventually, just like she would start eating healthy again eventually, and start exercising again when she wasn't bone-tired at the end of each day.

Came over to see if you needed any more help this week, he wrote on the notepad, holding it up so she could read it. Her eyes flicked over his now-familiar handwriting quickly.

"I don't think so," she said slowly, mentally going over the checklist of everything they still had to do. She took his offer seriously. They couldn't pay him, not yet, but he knew that, and she was sure he would be willing to work something out with them. "We're just putting the rest of the rooms together at this point, then we've got to wait for the inspection. Then we'll be ready to open."

He must have heard the nervousness in her voice, because he wrote, *Tourists won't know this place's history. You'll get guests.*

"I hope so," she said with a sigh.

It felt good to have someone to talk to besides Penny. She loved the woman like a sister, but after weeks of her only real conversation being with her, it felt like they had fallen into a pattern of spiraling into their worries together before trying desperately to convince themselves things would be all right after all. Sam's assurance was steadying. It made her wish she had more time to get to know him — since he needed his hands free to write, they couldn't exactly chat while he was working. Even though he lived in a house on the motel's property and she had been here for weeks, she barely knew anything about him.

"Actually," she said, accidentally interrupting him just as he put the pen to paper to write something else. "There's something I might be able to use your help with."

She gestured for him to follow her and opened the door to the kennel. Rosco and Luna began carrying on immediately at the sight of a stranger, though at the far end of the row of kennels, Cleo was as quiet and polite as ever. She opened Jasper's kennel, and he ran inside to get some water. Leaving him in there temporarily, she led Sam down to the far end and nodded down at Cleo, who sat watching them with her intelligent brown eyes.

"Do you remember seeing this dog around town at all?" she asked. Cleo was unique looking enough that she thought anyone who had seen her before would recognize her, and she knew she was right when Sam nodded.

Seen her walking with a woman a few times, he wrote. *Sometimes a man, too. Why?*

"I'll tell you in a second. First, what did the man look like? The woman too, I guess."

She waited impatiently while he wrote on his notepad, then held it out to her. She took it, reading the paragraph. *The man was tall, looked like he lifted weights. The woman was blonde, about your height.*

She chewed her lip as she read over the description. It didn't sound like the man was the same one who had dropped Cleo off. That didn't *necessarily* mean the dog was stolen, but it made it more likely, especially if she assumed the two people Sam usually saw Cleo walking with were her owners.

"Thanks," she said, handing the notepad back to him. "Want to hang out while I get the dogs' dinners ready? I'll tell you what happened earlier."

CHAPTER FOUR

Sam didn't have any more leads on who Cleo's real owners were, other than that he was pretty sure they lived in town, but he didn't dismiss her concerns, either. He promised to let her know if he saw the woman again, and she felt a bit better when he left. At least she had another person who agreed the circumstances around Cleo's drop-off were suspicious. Penny agreed with her too, but her friend was high-strung enough that she latched on to any worries Sadie shared with her. Having a third opinion made her feel less like she was overreacting, and more like something might actually be wrong.

She slept fitfully through the night with Jasper's warm weight curled in the crook of her legs, and her phone an arm's length away in case any of the cameras alerted her to movement. She closed the doggy doors between the indoor and outdoor portions of the runs at night to make sure no critters could come along and bother the dogs, and all of the doors were locked, but having a potentially stolen and very expensive dog on the property had her wound up like a spring.

In the morning, she cared for the dogs first thing, opening the sliding barriers to give them access to the outside again and doling out breakfast before she went back upstairs to make herself some coffee. Jasper ate his own meal up there with her, a certain smugness on his face as if he felt special for being with her while the other dogs were stuck in kennels.

After finishing her coffee, she went back down to the lobby in time to touch base with Penny before her friend left on a breakfast run. While Penny went out to get breakfast sandwiches, Sadie locked the dogs in the outdoors runs and mopped up the indoor kennels, washing dog fur and stray pieces of kibble down the drain before she refreshed the dogs' bedding and water. She had been feeding Cleo Jasper's food, since the man who dropped her off hadn't left her any, and thankfully, it seemed to be agreeing with her.

After raising the doggy door barriers again to let the dogs go in and out as they pleased, she went outside to pick up messes in the runs. Finally finished with her morning chores, she stopped in the lobby to email Rosco and Luna's owners their daily update, with new pictures of each dog attached. Only then did she return upstairs, Jasper by her side, to shower and change into cleaner clothes. Running a boarding kennel wasn't glamorous, but it was work she found satisfying, even the parts that were just cleaning.

Penny had left her breakfast sandwich on the lobby counter, and she gulped it down cold before dropping Jasper off in his kennel and finding Penny in Room Eight, where she was arranging toiletries in the bathroom. They were almost done with the room when she heard someone turn into the parking lot a couple of hours later. She peeked through the doorway to see a delivery van — the microchip scanner she had ordered had arrived.

"I'll be right back," she called over her shoulder as she hurried out to intercept the delivery man.

He handed the package over, and she took it with a thanks before hurrying into the lobby to unbox the scanner. After spending a few minutes reading the directions, she carried the device — which was an oblong device with a hoop on the end — back into the kennels. Cleo had been lying on her bed, but jumped up when she saw Sadie, her tail wagging.

"Hey, sweetie," Sadie said as she unlatched the door. She let Cleo sniff her and spent a few moments stroking the dog's silky fur — her fingers caught on a tangle, and she knew she would need to at least run a comb through the dog's coat later in order to keep it from becoming a tangled mess during her stay — before she turned the scanner on and waved it over the spot between her shoulder blades.

She was prepared to scan the dog's whole body if she had to — microchips migrated sometimes and could end up almost anywhere — but the scanner beeped right away. A number came up on the screen; proof that the dog had been chipped. Sadie patted Cleo's side.

"Good girl," she said as she stood up. "You wait here. I'm going to see if I can track down your real owner."

She latched the kennel and returned to the lobby where Penny's laptop was waiting. With painstaking care, she typed the number on the scanner into the most popular pet microchip registry, and once again she got lucky; Cleo's information popped up right away.

The first thing she noted was that the dog hadn't been reported as missing, not yet anyway. Her owner might not think of the microchip right away, so it wasn't a surefire way to tell whether her suspicions were right. Sadie took her phone out to type the owner's name — Melody Alma — along with her phone number and address. The address was a local one, though she wasn't familiar enough with the town to know where exactly in Greencreek it was.

She breathed out slowly as she dialed the phone number, trying to figure out what to say. *Hi, some shady guy dropped your dog off and I wanted to make sure he didn't steal her from you?* If the man who dropped Cleo off was a friend or family member of Melody's, that would just offend her. Maybe she should just lead with asking for more information about Cleo; a reasonable request, considering how little the man had said when he dropped her off.

In the end, it didn't matter what she planned to say, because as soon as the call went through, she was met with a dial tone and a robotic voice telling her *"Sorry, this number is no longer in service."*

"Darn it," she muttered, glancing down at the phone to check that she had typed the number in correctly. She had, which meant the number must be an old one, and Melody had forgotten to update Cleo's microchip when she got a new one.

A quick check on her phone's navigation app showed her that the address belonged to a building that was in downtown Greencreek, right along Main Street. A ten minute drive away.

It only took her a second to make the decision. She rose to her feet and left the lobby to find Penny vacuuming Room Eight. Her friend shut the machine off when Sadie waved at her.

"Any luck?"

"Sort of," Sadie said. "She has a chip, but the number it's registered to is old. Her owner's name is Melody Alma, and it looks like she lives here in Greencreek. Her address might be an old one too, but I'd like to check it out anyway. Do you want to come with me?"

"No way am I letting you go alone," Penny said. "Give me five minutes. As soon as I finish vacuuming, this room will be ready. That will be the perfect time for a break."

Less than ten minutes later, Sadie was behind the wheel of her SUV with Penny in the passenger seat next to her, the air conditioning blowing at them full blast. Penny's hair — dyed a deep red, her friend's favorite color — was pulled back in a messy ponytail, the pale red roots showing. Penny had always been the sort to keep her hair, nails, and makeup picture perfect, and the lapse was a sign that Sadie hadn't been the only one working herself to the bone.

"Hopefully this pans out and the mystery of Cleo is one more thing we can check off our list," she said as Sadie drove them into town. "How's she doing? She's such a gorgeous dog. I need to go say hi to her when we get back."

"She's been perfect," Sadie said. "I can tell someone really loves her, which is why this is so weird. What's the address again?"

While Penny read it off to her, Sadie slowed. Finally, she pulled to a stop along the curb in front of a furniture store with advertisements pasted in the windows that looked like they hadn't been updated in a decade. It wasn't the furniture store she was looking for, though; it was the narrow door that led up to the apartment above it. She double checked the address she had noted down in her phone, but this was it; this was where Cleo's owner lived. Sadie couldn't imagine owning such a large breed dog in an apartment in the middle of town where there was barely even any grass for the dog to do its business on, but she supposed it would be doable if Melody put in the work to keep Cleo happy.

They got out of the SUV together, but Sadie was the one who led the way to the door, Penny lagging further behind with every step. Penny hated confrontation, and while she had gotten better at it over the years — seven years spent in hospitality work had at least given her the power to stand up to irate guests — she still preferred to let Sadie take the lead when something looked like it was going to be unpleasant.

That meant Sadie was the one to press the buzzer, and when there was no answer, she was the one who tried the door and found it unlocked.

"What are you doing?" Penny hissed as Sadie pushed the door open. It led to a narrow staircase, which ended at another door that led into the apartment proper.

"Maybe the buzzer's broken," Sadie whispered back. "I want to at least try knocking."

She climbed up the stairs as quietly as she could, blaming her sudden tension on Penny's worried breaths behind her. She cleared her throat when she reached the top and raised her fist to knock on the door, only to pause when she saw that it was already open a crack. There was a metallic smell in the air; not strong, but enough that she noticed it now that she was paying attention, and something that smelled like fireworks. Gunpowder.

"Don't," Penny whispered, but Sadie was already reaching for the door. Ignoring her, she pushed it open. The first thing she spotted was a fancy metal dog bowl on the kitchen floor with Cleo's name etched into the side. She took a step inside, then froze as her eyes landed on a pair of boots sticking out from behind the counter that divided the kitchen from the living room.

Boots that were attached to a pair of jean-clad legs. A body. She got one look at the tall, dark-haired man, then she saw the blood congealing on the tiles around him and spun around, stumbling back onto the landing with Penny, who was already gagging.

CHAPTER FIVE

The police response was quick, but Sheriff Islington looked skeptical when he stepped out of his cruiser. He was a tall, narrow, man with a goatee, who looked more like a villain than someone who was supposed to be a hero; Sadie had spoken to him a few times when the murder happened at their motel, and she knew he wasn't as intimidating as he looked, but he seemed to carry a healthy dose of suspicion about everything.

"Got a call about a body?" he said as he approached, his thumb tucked behind the belt that held his revolver. He looked between them, his brow furrowing in a way that told her he recognized them. "Paramedics are a few minutes out yet."

"Yes!" Penny said. She was clinging to Sadie's arm, and Sadie clung back, trying not to let the image of the man lying on the kitchen floor creep back into her mind. "He's up there."

"You two sit tight," he told them as he started up the narrow, enclosed staircase. As he vanished from sight, Sadie managed to tug her friend over to a shaded spot under one of the few trees planted by the sidewalk.

They didn't have to wait long for Sheriff Islington to come back down. His expression was more serious now; if he suspected the call was a prank or an overreaction before, he had now realized it was deadly real.

He gestured at them to wait while he flagged down the ambulance and spoke to the paramedics. He must have called for backup at some point, because a deputy arrived not long after and strung crime scene tape across the door while the sheriff and the paramedics went upstairs. They had to duck under the tape when they came back down; the paramedics left without the body.

The sheriff conversed with his deputy for a moment before he strolled over to them and took a notebook out of his pocket; the same kind Sam used,

Sadie realized. The unimportant thought made her realize she was probably in shock.

"Sadie Barton and Penelope Montgomery," he drawled. "I wasn't expecting to see the two of you again anytime soon. Y'all doing all right out at that motel?"

Penny nodded, her jaw clenched and her face pale. Sadie spoke up for both of them. "Yes, sir. We haven't had any other problems until... well, until yesterday."

He raised an eyebrow. "Does yesterday's 'problem' have something to do with this, or do you need to make a separate report?"

"I think it has something to do with this," Sadie said.

"Then start talkin'. I'm all ears."

She told him about Cleo's drop-off, and the suspicious looking man who brought her to the kennel, then with Penny chiming in whenever she could, told him how that ended up leading them here.

When she finished, she showed him the security video of the man who dropped Cleo off. The camera's angle wasn't the best; it was hard to see anything besides his ball cap and sunglasses, but he made a note of the model of the station wagon.

"I'd appreciate it if you can email me that video," he said, passing her a business card. "And any other footage you might have of him or his vehicle. It doesn't look like our victim is the same man as the one on the camera, which means he might be our suspect."

"Of course. I'll do it as soon as I get back to the motel."

He glanced at his watch. "I'd like to stop by and take a look at that dog, too. It might be a couple hours until I'm done here. Will one of you be around?"

They exchanged a glance. "We should be," Sadie said.

He nodded, then took a step back and tipped his hat to them. "Y'all get home safe. And keep this to yourselves for now. Greencreek doesn't see many homicides. I don't want people to panic."

They drove home together, panicking.

"It was one thing when we thought she might be stolen, but this is murder, Sadie. What if we end up like that guy?"

"We won't," Sadie said, her knuckles white around the wheel.

"How do you know?"

"All we're doing is boarding a dog. There's no reason for someone to target us."

"What if that guy who dropped her off is the killer?" Penny leaned across the gap between the seats, lowering her voice. "He's going to come back."

"I know," Sadie hissed, risking a glance over at her. "But what am I supposed to do about it? I can't just drop her off at the pound."

"I know," Penny said. "Jeez. I wasn't going to suggest that. The poor thing would be terrified. But we need to try to find someone else to take her. We should look Melody up online and see if she has a social media profile or something."

"That was her apartment. She might be in trouble. Or she might be trouble."

Penny let out a groan and leaned her head back against the seat. "Great. Just great. You ever wonder if the motel is cursed? We're not the first ones who have had a string of bad luck there."

"I don't think we're the ones who had bad luck this time," Sadie said.

"Right." Her friend grimaced. "That poor guy. I wonder who he was. I didn't get a good look at him, did you?"

"Tall, dark-haired... that's about it. Sheriff Islington was right; he's definitely not the same guy who dropped Cleo off."

"I don't like this," Penny said. "I hope you're

right, and the killer won't come looking for us because we have Cleo. We'll just have to keep our heads down and hope trouble passes us by this time."

Sheriff Islington didn't make it out to the motel until early evening. He looked tired, and Sadie felt a surge of empathy for him. Stumbling across the scene of a murder had been bad enough for them, but he was the one who had to deal with the aftermath, as well as carry the weight of the responsibility of keeping the town safe.

"The place looks better," he said, glancing around the lobby. "Where's that dog?"

"I'll bring you back to her," Sadie said, rising from the uncomfortable chair where she had been sitting. Penny had claimed the more comfortable rolling chair behind the counter and was busy filling out one of the many forms they needed to complete prior to being able to open. "It's going to be loud, brace yourself."

He patted Jasper, who had been enjoying their down time in the lobby with his favorite ball, and followed her through the laundry room and into the kennels, where Rosco and Luna greeted them with barks and howls. In the first kennel, Cleo got up from her bed and walked over to the chain link door to greet Sadie.

"That's a pretty dog," the sheriff said, looking down at her. "I checked before I came here; we still don't have any reports that she's missing or stolen. She friendly?"

"She has been so far, but I don't know anything about her," Sadie said. "She seems very well trained."

He opened the kennel and stepped inside, letting Cleo sniff him before he looked her over. "Did she have any injuries or anything in her fur? Blood?"

"No. I looked her over well. She seems healthy, and she was immaculately groomed."

"Did she have a collar when she arrived?" he asked as he stepped out of the kennel.

She nodded and showed it to him. "She had a collar and leash, but no tags. That's all, plus her records and five hundred dollars in cash."

"Do you have that handy?" He must have seen the reluctant expression on her face, because he said, "If you do, I need to take it in as evidence, but I'll make sure you get it back if it turns out to be the wrong lead."

She sighed. "Yeah. We kept it separate."

She watched as he took a photo of Cleo for evidence, then walked back into the lobby with him, where Penny fetched the envelope of cash and the photocopy of Cleo's records. He let Sadie take a picture of the latter, then zipped both into plastic bags. The sight of the evidence bags made it feel official; they might have unknowingly had a brush with the killer already.

CHAPTER SIX

They decided to lock up for the evening after the sheriff left. Dinner was frozen dinners; they microwaved them in Sadie's kitchen above the lobby and brought Penny's laptop upstairs so they could try to track down Melody while they ate on the couch.

"No, you get dinner with the others," Sadie said, pushing Jasper's questing nose back as she sat down with her microwaved pasta. "I'm not sharing."

"I'll share," Penny said. She picked a potato out of her tray and blew on it briefly before tossing it to him. He snapped it out of the air before Sadie could say anything.

"This is why he's still begging," she grumbled. "He knows you're an easy mark."

"He knows he can rely on his auntie to feed him when he's starving, you mean."

"He just had a dental chew." Sadie rolled her eyes and set her food down on the coffee table — it was too hot to eat right away. Jasper looked down at it, his floppy ears perked up, then realized she was staring at him and went to go lay on his bed. "Good boy."

"Let's get started," Penny said. She propped the laptop on top of a pillow between them and turned the computer toward Sadie. "You search while I eat. Then we'll switch."

Sadie nodded and pulled up the web browser, navigating to the most popular social media website; Penny's profile was already logged in. She ignored the myriad of notifications her friend had — she couldn't stand having a single unread message, but Penny was the complete opposite — and typed Melody Alma's name into the search bar.

She was easy to find; Cleo's long muzzle peered back at Sadie from her profile picture. She clicked on the profile, but there wasn't much to see. Melody seemed to have it completely locked down — she didn't even have the option to send her a message.

"All you can see is her tagged pictures," Penny complained. "It's smart, of course, but when people set their profiles to private, it makes snooping so much harder."

"Maybe we can find someone in her tagged photos who can contact her for us," Sadie said.

"We don't even know if she's alive," Penny said. "And what if we reach out to the wrong person? We have no idea who's involved in this, or even what 'this' is."

"We could try family, her mom or a sibling maybe. Someone who might know whether she's safe." She paused. "Or who might be willing to take Cleo."

Someone else taking the dog didn't sit quite right with her, but she didn't know what else to do. The thought of letting Cleo go with that stranger when he came to pick her up didn't sit right either. Not when, for all they knew, he was the one who killed the man in Melody's apartment and might be the reason Melody was missing. Finding a close family member of Melody's seemed like the safest bet, and she was sure they would appreciate knowing Cleo was safe, too.

They began scrolling through her tagged photos, but to Sadie's disappointment, didn't find anyone who shared a last name with her. From the looks of it, Melody hadn't been tagged in very many photos lately. There was one posted a couple of weeks ago of her at a lake with Cleo by her side, and a tall, dark-haired man next to her, his arm around her waist. As soon as she saw him, Sadie froze.

"What is it?" Penny asked.

"That's him," Sadie said. "That's the man who was in the apartment. The... victim."

Penny set her food down so she could lean close to the screen. "Dang it, there are a few people tagged in the photo," she said. "I don't know which one he is."

She clicked on one of the names, then backed out when it led her to the wrong person's profile. The next name she clicked on, Damien Montrose, brought up a profile picture, a close-up of the victim's face. Sadie hadn't gotten a good look at him, but she was absolutely certain it was the same man. He had dark, medium-length hair, a Roman nose, and was tall enough that it stood out in every picture where he was with someone else.

There had been nothing posted on his page yet about his death, but Sadie knew they had found the right person.

"Who was he?" she asked. "I mean, in relation to Melody?"

"I don't know. Her boyfriend, I guess?" Penny

said as she scrolled down his page. He didn't post very much either, but there was one other picture of him with Melody. The two of them standing under an orange streetlight at night, their arms wrapped around each other. The photo made it clear that Penny's guess was right — the two of them must have been together.

"So... Melody's boyfriend was shot to death in her own apartment, and a stranger dropped her dog off with us," Sadie said slowly. "What's going on?"

"I don't know, but I don't like it," Penny said. She backed out of Melody's profile and continued looking through the tagged photos. "Do any of these people look like the guy who dropped Cleo off?"

Sadie peered at the images as her friend scrolled past, but most of the photos seemed to be of Melody and her female friends... at least up until a month ago. Before that, there were a lot of pictures of her with a tall, muscular, blond man, the sight of whom jogged something in her memory.

"Hang on," she said, tapping the screen. "Sam said he'd seen Melody walking Cleo with a man who matched this description."

"His name is Ford Jackson," Penny said, finding one of the photos he was tagged in. "Looks like he's her ex or something." She scrolled down his profile until she came to a photo memory which Melody had been tagged in. "Aww, it's baby Cleo," she said, showing Sadie the photo from three years ago. "She's adorable."

"She's the cutest," Sadie crooned. "Look at her fluff. I bet she was so soft. It looks like this Ford guy gave her to Melody as a gift."

"They must have been together for a while," Penny said. "You don't give someone a dog as a gift unless you're serious about them."

"You shouldn't give someone a dog as a gift at all," Sadie muttered, but it seemed to have turned out alright for Cleo, so she couldn't be too upset in this case.

She stared at Ford's picture for a few seconds longer. As the ex, he had to be a person of interest in Damien's murder, but he was definitely not the thin, shorter man who had dropped Cleo off. If they wanted to get to the bottom of things, tracking him down seemed almost as important as tracking Melody down was. He was the only person she was certain would have answers.

CHAPTER SEVEN

Sadie spent another restless night listening for the chime of a notification from the security cameras, but none came, and when she went downstairs in the morning, all three of the dogs she was boarding were happy, safe, excited for breakfast. She went through her normal routine of feeding them and cleaning the kennels. When she finished, she sipped coffee while she looked for more news about Damien's murder online. There were a couple of posts in the town's social media group made by people who were trying to figure out what was going on, but no one seemed to know more than she already did. The one bright side was that there was no mention of the motel. Hopefully, she and Penny would be able to keep their names out of this one.

They worked on Rooms Eight and Nine until late morning, when they decided to make a run into town to pick up takeout from the diner for lunch and to stop by the hardware store for a new box of drywall anchors. If it wasn't for the mystery surrounding Cleo and her missing owner, Sadie thought today might have been one of the best days they'd had since they moved to Greencreek. They were now so close to opening the motel portion of their business that she could taste it.

They stopped at the diner first, picking up their to-go order of a chicken salad sandwich for Penny and a BLT for Sadie, both with sides of crispy fries and an impulse-bought half an apple pie to share. Their next stop was the hardware store, where they grabbed the drywall anchors and screws, and a welcome mat for the lobby — it was on sale, and they needed one anyway — before going to the counter to check out. Sadie and Penny had been coming in frequently enough that the owner, an elderly woman named Norma Underwood, recognized them on sight.

"It's lovely to see you, as always, dears," she said as she manually typed the prices into the register, then bagged the items. "No Jasper today?"

"No, we had a few stops to make, and we didn't want to leave him in the car," Sadie said as she reached into her purse for her wallet. She was running on empty, but Penny had paid for their lunch, and it wasn't fair to expect her friend to cover everything.

"I'm sure he's sad he's missing out," Norma said. "You go on and bring a treat home for him."

"Oh, thank you," Sadie said. She opened the glass jar and took out one of the dog treats. "He'll appreciate it."

"Anytime. And you make sure you bring him next time. He's a lovely dog."

"Do a lot of people bring their dogs in?" Penny asked.

"Oh, yes," Norma said. "I always encourage it when I learn someone has a pet. It brightens my day whenever I peek over the counter to see a furry little face smiling back up at me."

At Penny's pointed look, Sadie took out her cell phone. Maybe they weren't as out of luck as she had thought. She kept forgetting how small Greencreek was. Cleo stood out enough that someone like Norma was bound to recognize her.

"Have you seen this dog before?" she asked. "Her name's Cleo."

"Oh, yes. That's Melody's sweet girl. Do you know her? I suppose you've heard what happened yesterday. So sad. A stranger was found murdered in

Melody's apartment and no one's seen hide nor hair of her or her dog." Norma's eyes narrowed as she looked at Cleo's photo. "Does this mean what I think it means? That sweet Cleo is safe and sound with the two of you?"

Sadie hesitated. It hadn't occurred to her that Norma would put it together, but she knew Sadie and Penny ran Sit, Stay, Sleep Motel and Boarding, and the background in the photo clearly was that of a kennel rather than someone's living room.

"We're watching her right now, but she's involved in the police investigation, so we'd like to keep it quiet," she said as she withdrew her phone and slipped it back into her purse.

"Mum's the word," Norma said. "Does that mean Sheriff Islington has spoken to the two of you? Does he have any idea what happened to Melody? She and her boyfriend used to come in quite often. He owns a gym, and he does all of the maintenance by himself. Come to think of it, I haven't seen them together for quite a while. She stopped coming in with him a few weeks ago, and he's seemed down ever since."

"By her boyfriend, do you mean the muscular blond guy?" Sadie asked. She accepted the receipt, and Penny grabbed the bag.

Norma nodded. "Ford Jackson. He's a very strapping young man. I always thought they were wonderful together, but now I'm beginning to wonder if they've broken up." She shook her head. "Oh, listen to me. I shouldn't gossip. I just hope Melody's safe. You two have a lovely day, now, and I hope next time you'll bring that handsome young hound in with you."

They decided to go to Sunshine Desserts next. Bailey, the young woman who owned the cookie shop, had been asking them for updates on how the motel was doing every time they stopped in. As soon as they had a little bit of extra spending money, they planned on getting regular deliveries of her cookies — both human and dog varieties — to sell at their motel. The little cookie shop was popular, and they had plenty of time to peer into the glass display cases and decide what they wanted while they waited for their turn at the register.

When they stepped up to the counter, Bailey greeted them with a bright smile. "Hey Sadie, Penny," she said. "What can I get the two of you?"

"I'll try that butterscotch delight cookie," Sadie said. "And I'd like four of your vanilla and carob sandwich cookies for the dogs."

"Coming right up," Bailey said. "And you?"

"I'll take the peppermint white chocolate cookie," Penny said.

"Anything else?" Bailey asked as she typed their order in.

Penny shook her head, but Sadie said, "Actually, do you know what kind of cookies Sam likes?"

"Sam Walker? I know he really likes these almond marzipan cookies," Bailey said, nodding toward the case where they were displayed. "Do you want one of those, too?"

"Yeah, I'll take one. He's been a real help at the motel, and we haven't been able to pay him properly. I figure bribing him with cookies can't hurt."

Bailey smiled as she typed the order in. "Will that be card or cash?"

Sadie paid again this time, mostly because she didn't want Penny to feel like she had to pay for Sam's cookie. Bailey placed their cookies in bags, keeping the dog cookies and human cookies separate. The people behind them in line were still trying to figure out what they wanted — they had a couple of young children with them who seemed to be arguing about what they wanted to split. After glancing at them to make sure they were still busy, she leaned conspiratorially across the counter and lowered her voice.

"Have the two of you heard about the murder yet? It's been the talk of the town all day."

"Oh, we heard about it," Penny said. "Did you know the guy?"

Bailey shook her head. "Damien? I didn't know him well. From what I heard, he was a troublemaker, dropped out of high school when he was younger, that sort of thing. I'm not sure anyone is too surprised he met with a messy end, but I'm shocked that it happened at Melody's apartment."

"Did you know her?"

"Melody? Yeah. We went to school together. We weren't super close, but she stops to chat whenever she comes in. She told me that she broke up with Ford and started dating Damien. I told her she was crazy, but that it wasn't any of my business."

"Do you think Ford could have had something to do with it?" Sadie asked, leaning forward. They were talking in whispers now, not wanting the children to overhear. "I gather she and him were serious. He might have some unpleasant feelings about her ending things with him for someone else."

"Ford? I don't know," Bailey said. "He's the golden retriever, gym-bro type. I know he adored Melody, so I suppose it could go either way. The whole situation is strange. She wasn't able to give me a good answer when I asked why she left Ford. I heard a rumor that Damien inherited some money, so maybe that was the motivation, but I never thought of Melody as the gold-digger type. Her brother, maybe. That man's crafty."

"Her brother?" Sadie said.

Bailey nodded. "Andrew. I actually knew him pretty well when we were younger. He was in my year back in high school."

"What does he look like?"

"Why the third degree about him?" Bailey asked, narrowing her eyes. "You both seem very interested in this."

"We'll tell you later," Sadie said. It sounded like the children behind them were coming to an agreement, which meant they had to hurry. "Just, if you had to describe him in a sentence or two?"

"Um. Short, I guess? Like, short for a guy; about your height, maybe. Kind of skinny. Intense. Not a bad guy, just a little weird, you know?"

"Excuse me, I think we're ready to order now."

Penny grabbed the cookies as Sadie said, "Thanks, Bailey. Seriously, stop by the motel anytime. We'll tell you what's going on."

Bailey nodded as she turned to her next

customers, clearly curious even if she couldn't pursue it right now.

"That's got to be him," Sadie muttered to her friend as they stepped onto the sidewalk. "I know it. The guy who dropped Cleo off was Melody's brother."

CHAPTER EIGHT

They went back to the motel to have their sandwiches while they went through the checklist of everything they still had to do to finish preparing the rooms. Neither of them felt like getting back to work right after eating, so Penny decided to start a load of laundry while Sadie took Jasper and the almond cookie over to Sam's house.

The narrow path between the motel and the little yellow house Sam rented from them had become noticeably more worn with foot traffic since they moved there. She liked the thought of one day installing an actual footpath, with stepping stones or some pretty rocks, but Sam might not like that. If it looked like an official path, their guests might decide to wander onto his property. For now, the narrow game trail would have to do.

Jasper trotted ahead of her, off-leash, and loped across Sam's neatly trimmed grass up to his porch, while she trailed behind. She didn't see his truck parked in the shade under the oak tree like she normally did and felt a pang of disappointment that she probably wasn't going to get to see him.

She tried knocking anyway, but the house remained silent, so she placed the paper bag with the cookie on the small table next to one of the rocking chairs on his porch before she turned to go. Even Jasper seemed disappointed that they weren't going to see Sam. He stood by the front door, looking back at her sadly as she descended the steps.

His ears perked up a second before she recognized the sound of someone turning onto the gravel driveway from the road. A moment later, Sam's old truck trundled into view. She called Jasper over before he could get in the way of the vehicle and snatched the bag with the cookie in it back up so she could hand it to him herself.

She raised a hand in greeting as he got out of his truck, then released Jasper so he could run over and say hi. She followed her dog at a more sedate pace. Sam made a motion with his hands, then reached back into his truck and scribbled on his notepad, *Sorry. What's up?*

"I brought you a cookie," she said. "Almond marzipan. Bailey said they're your favorite." He raised an eyebrow but reached out to take it, and she started talking again before he had to write his question down. "Just a thanks for all the help you've been doing."

He nodded, then quickly scribbled a note. *Did you ever find out what's going on with that dog?*

She shook her head. "Not exactly. We've been asking around, though. If you've got time, I'll tell you what we learned."

He nodded, so she leaned against the truck next to him and accepted a piece of the cookie that he handed to her. It was good; not a flavor she would normally have tried, but she liked its subtle sweetness. Jasper sniffed along the edge of Sam's yard as she told him everything they had learned.

When she finished, he asked, *Do you think it's safe to be asking questions?*

"I don't know," she admitted. "We let slip to Norma that we have Cleo, and I wish we hadn't. But I feel like I have to do something. I hate the thought of that guy, I'm almost certain he's Andrew Alma, Melody's brother — coming back to pick Cleo up before we have a chance to contact Melody. We still don't even know if Melody is even alive." She bit her lip. "I guess... I feel a duty to make sure Cleo goes home with the right person."

Do you need help?

"I don't think there's anything you could do," she said. "For now, we're going to have to sit tight. I've been keeping an eye on the security cameras, and we're making sure we lock everything up at night. He did say he wouldn't be back for a week or two, so we've got some time. Hopefully, Sheriff Islington will have figured out what's going on by then."

Call if you need anything, he wrote. *Or shout. I'll bring my axe.*

She let out a huff of laughter and pushed away from the truck. "Thanks. It makes me feel better knowing you're here. Same goes for you. I don't think anyone will give you trouble, but you are right next door to the motel. If anyone hassles you about Cleo, just let me know."

She raised a hand in a wave, promised to see him later, then called Jasper to her side and left him to finish his cookie in peace while she returned to the motel. Penny was waiting for her in the lobby, folding clean clothes out of a hamper. They would have to stop using the lobby as their hangout space eventually, but for now, it was a convenient place to spend time together when they weren't busy.

"How's Sam?" Penny asked as Sadie joined her. "Did he appreciate the cookie? Did he try to thank you with a kiss?" She fluttered her eyelashes dramatically, and Sadie made a rude gesture in response.

"It's not like that. I told you; I wanted to thank him for all his help."

"Uh-huh," her friend said. "Right."

"I've got way too much to do to even think of dating," Sadie said, rolling her eyes. "I'm going to go check on the dogs, then I'll help you work on the rooms a little more. Think we'll finish tonight?"

"Probably not tonight," Penny said. "But we might be able to get it done tomorrow."

With that news to bolster her, she took Jasper back into the kennels with her. Cleo came over to greet her, and Sadie scratched her chin through the chain link. Luna was so excited she began to howl, and Rosco did his usual pogo stick jumping, straight up and down. Sadie ushered Jasper into the last kennel and made sure everyone had fresh water, then she took Luna out to brush her again. The husky was still shedding like crazy.

"I'll have to do you next, Cleo," she said. "Your

owner won't be happy if she picks you up and your gorgeous fur is a matted mess."

Her phone chimed with a notification from the security camera app, but she had her hands full of energetic husky, so she ignored it, trusting Penny would handle it. Less than a minute later, her friend poked her head through the door to the laundry room. Sadie knew as soon as she saw her face that something was wrong.

What is it?" she asked, grabbing Luna before the husky could dart into the laundry room.

"Someone is here asking about a dog." Her voice was casual, but she widened her eyes and gave Cleo a very pointed look. "I told him you were the one that handled all of that."

Worried, Sadie put Luna back in her kennel and slipped through the door into the laundry room. In the brief moment of privacy before she stepped into the lobby, she pulled Penny aside.

"Who is it?" she whispered.

"It's her ex," Penny whispered back. "Ford."

She took a deep breath. Ford had to be a suspect; she couldn't risk him realizing they had Cleo.

"Will you put Cleo into the outdoor run and lower the barriers so she can't get back in? Then put all of her bedding…" she trailed off, looking around for a hiding place. "Stuff it in one of the washers, I guess. Make sure you hide her collar and leash, too. When you're done, call the sheriff and let him know someone's here looking for Cleo."

Her friend gave her a tight nod and slipped back into the kennel room while Sadie stepped into the lobby.

CHAPTER NINE

The man waiting for her in the lobby looked like every little girl's dream of Prince Charming. Tall and blond, with arm muscles that told Sadie he probably lifted more than she and Penny weighed combined, and warm blue eyes. He gave her a polite smile that didn't quite reach them as he turned toward her.

"Hi. Sadie?" he asked.

"That's me," she said, giving him a polite customer service smile. She hoped he couldn't tell how fast her heart was pounding. Why was he here? How had he found them?

"I hope you can help me. Your coworker said you're the one who handles the boarding side of the business. My name is Ford Jackson, and I'm looking for a dog I believe might have been stolen." He tapped on his phone to wake up the screen, then turned it toward her. "Her name is Cleo, and she's a purebred Afghan hound."

"She's beautiful," Sadie said as she glanced at the picture. She felt a flicker of doubt as she looked at him. It was hard to imagine this man was the killer, but she couldn't ignore the fact that it was his ex-girlfriend who was missing and his ex-girlfriend's new boyfriend who was dead. "Is there a reason you believe she might be here?"

"I'm checking with every animal-related business in the area," he said. "Do you mind if I take a peek in your kennels? Someone may have dropped her off under a different name or might have given her a haircut trying to hide her. I've known her since she was a puppy. She'll recognize me."

"Is she your dog?" Sadie asked.

He shook his head. "No, she's… a close friend's dog. You might have heard of the shooting that took place in town? Well, it happened in my friend's apartment and she and her dog have both been missing for the past few days. Her name is Melody Alma. She was last seen with her brother, Andrew Alma. I've already spoken to the police, and I believe it's a possible kidnapping. I know Melody wouldn't leave her dog behind voluntarily, but if something happened, it's possible someone might have found her and picked her up. She's a very expensive breed, so the possibility of intentional theft is there, too. I'd feel much better being able to confirm for myself that she isn't here."

Warning bells went off in Sadie's mind. If he really had spoken to the police about Cleo, wouldn't Sheriff Islington have at least told him the dog was safe?

"Yes, right this way," she said.

Turning away from him to hide the expression on her face, she gestured for Ford to follow her. All she could do was hope that Penny was done hiding evidence that Cleo was there. She led him through the laundry room, then back into the kennels, where Penny was nowhere to be seen, and neither was Cleo. Cleo's kennel was empty, and Sadie could see that the barrier separating the indoor kennel from the outdoor run was down. They left all of the unoccupied kennels closed to the outside, so she didn't think that would stand out to him.

"We only have two guests at the moment," she said to Ford, leading him past Cleo's empty kennel. He glanced in briefly before moving on to the next one. "And I can promise you neither Luna nor Rosco are Afghan hounds. The dog at the very end is Jasper, my foxhound."

He peered into each kennel. When he turned back to her, the smile on his face seemed a little more genuine. "Thank you for this. I feel much better knowing I can cross this place off my list. Can I email you a picture of her and ask you to call me if you do see her?"

"Of course," Sadie said. "I hope your friend's all right."

"Thank you," he said. "Me too."

She escorted him back into the lobby, where she wrote the motel's email address down on a sticky note for him — they hadn't gotten around to printing out business cards yet. She followed him to the door when he left and peered out through the window, not breathing a sigh of relief until she saw his vehicle — a shiny new pickup truck — pull out of the parking lot.

As soon as he had vanished down the road, she hurried into the kennel room and went out through the back door, where she found Penny by the outdoor runs. She was crouched outside of Cleo's kennel, petting the dog through the chain link, with her other hand pressing her phone to her ear.

"Is he gone?" she asked, standing up, much to Cleo's disappointment.

"Yeah, he just left," Sadie said. "I think it worked. He didn't know she was here."

"Thank goodness. I'm on the phone with the sheriff's department right now. They want to know if they should send someone out."

"I don't think there's anything they could do," Sadie said. "Sheriff Islington should know that Ford came here looking for her, though."

Penny nodded and resumed speaking to the person on the other end of the line. Sadie walked back along the row of kennels, all three of the other dogs rushing outside to join them. Luna and Rosco were going bananas — it was about time for their daily walk through the woods, and they seemed to know it.

She took a deep breath and forced her shoulders to relax. Ford had left, and from the sound of it, this had just been a routine check. He didn't know Cleo was here, and he had no reason to come back. The disaster had been averted.

CHAPTER TEN

Luna's owner came to pick her up bright and early the next morning. Sadie managed to finish brushing her before she arrived, and made sure all of Luna's bedding was fresh and clean and ready to go home with her. The husky was thrilled to see her owner and ran in huge circles around the lobby while the woman counted out her cash.

"Thank you so much for taking care of her. How was she?"

"She was great," Sadie said. "I think she was a little stressed on the first night, but she seemed to settle in quickly. We'd love to have her back whenever you need to go out of town again."

"I appreciate that. It's great to know that there's a

place like this where we can drop her off whenever we need someone to watch her."

Sadie tucked the cash into their cash register, relieved to have a little more money on hand, even if it wasn't much. Then she said a final goodbye to Luna and waved from the lobby door as she and her owner got into their vehicle.

She and Penny spent the rest of the morning putting the finishing touches on Rooms Nine and Ten. They had saved Room Ten for last, both because it was the last in the row and also because neither of them liked that room very much. It was the site of a string of gruesome murders, the last of which had taken place only a few weeks ago. They had spent too much money getting the room professionally cleaned after tearing the carpet out, and now no one could tell what had happened just by looking at it, but Sadie could have sworn that the temperature was always a few degrees colder than the other rooms. She knew it was all in her head, but she still felt guilty at the thought of guests staying there.

"We'll have to hang a laminated No Pets sign for now," Penny said, as they made the bed together. "We should order a nice-looking one when we have the money, though."

"Yeah, we'll add it to the list of everything else

we need to buy," Sadie said with a sigh. "I can't believe this is it. As soon as we pass the inspection, we'll be ready to open to guests."

They tucked the comforter in together, then stood back and looked around. The room was done. It was the only pet-free room they were going to offer; they both wanted to have space for guests with allergies, but with the dog training business attached to the motel, most of their target demographic was pet owners.

"Yeah, this is it."

They exchanged a look. After weeks of work, it was strange to think they were finally done renovating the rooms. The motel still needed a lot of work, but as long as they passed the inspection, they were ready to open.

"We should celebrate," Penny said after a second. "I bought some champagne just for this."

"You don't think we should wait until after the inspection?"

"Don't worry, I have another bottle for then," her friend said with a wink. "Do you have to do anything with the dogs?"

"I should go check on them," Sadie said. "Meet you in the lobby in about ten minutes?"

"Sounds good to me."

Sadie hurried back to the kennel to check on Jasper, Rosco, and Cleo. Rosco's owner was supposed to pick him up later, then it would be just the two dogs. She made sure everyone had fresh water, then let Jasper out of his kennel and brought him into the lobby with her.

Penny was already waiting with a bottle of champagne and two flutes. She popped the cork as Sadie joined her and poured the foaming drink into the champagne flutes. She held one out to Sadie, then raised her own in a toast.

"To our new business adventure," she said. "We're going to make this work."

Sadie raised her glass and clinked it against Penny's, then sipped her champagne. They had both known this wouldn't be easy, but the motel had taken much more work to get to this point than she expected. It felt good to finally be done, but it was just one worry to check off of a long list of them. Cleo's situation was at the top, but one way or another, that would be resolved within the next week or two.

The longer-term matter of staying afloat weighed on her more heavily. They couldn't keep going with just a handful of boarding clients each week. She needed to get her training business up and running, but she didn't want to get overwhelmed with opening the motel at the same time. She and Penny would just have to hope they got a lot of guests from the get-go.

"Oh, this is good stuff," Penny said. She turned the bottle to look at the label. "I like it. I don't think I've bought it before. Do you want more?"

"Sure," Sadie said as she drained her flute. It was a celebration, after all. Just because they weren't done yet didn't mean they hadn't worked hard to get as far as they had. She held her glass out while Penny refilled it.

When her phone chimed, she took it out of her pocket and checked the screen. It was a notification from the security camera app; a person had been detected on the back camera that looked out over the kennel runs.

"What is it?" Penny asked, after seeing the look on her face.

"I don't know," Sadie said. "It's probably just a…"

She trailed off as she played the video clip and saw that it wasn't a raccoon or a bird that the camera misidentified. It really was a person. A woman, with her hair pulled back into a ponytail and dark sunglasses over her eyes. She was standing near Cleo's kennel run, and Cleo was racing back and forth in excitement, more lively than Sadie had seen her yet.

The video clip ended, and she quickly switched to the live feed. But the woman — Melody, it had to be Melody — was gone.

She raced into the kennels and out through the back door, both Penny and Jasper hurrying behind her. Rosco began barking as she passed by his kennel, then followed her out into the run behind the building. Cleo was still outside; Sadie saw with a rush of relief. She wagged her tail when she spotted the three of them approach, then looked past Sadie with a sad whine.

Sadie turned around, but there was no one there. "She's not back here anymore. Let's check in the front."

"Sadie, what's going on?" Penny asked as they jogged around the building.

"I think I just saw Melody on the camera. She was back here with Cleo."

Just as they rounded the corner of the building, Sadie heard tires screech and saw a station wagon that had been pulled up along the shoulder in front of the motel speed away. She got a glimpse of two people inside — one, the woman she had just seen with Cleo, and the other, the man who had dropped Cleo off — before the station wagon vanished down the road.

Sadie was dialing the sheriff's number even

before they turned to go back inside. She didn't know what Melody and her brother had been doing here, but she had them on camera, and she fully intended to turn the footage in. She was glad that Melody looked like she was all right, but she didn't appreciate that the missing woman had dragged the motel into whatever was going on.

CHAPTER ELEVEN

"I'll send a few extra patrols by," Sheriff Islington said. He was already halfway out the door. "They'll keep an eye out for you."

Sadie knew he was busy, and it wasn't as if Greencreek was crawling with enough bored sheriff's deputies that he could leave parked outside their door the entire time, but she wished he could do something more than take their security footage and promise to keep an eye on things.

"That's it?" Penny asked, echoing her thoughts. "Melody was just here, and we had to deal with Ford before that. Who knows who will be next?"

"The only other thing I can offer is to take the dog to the county shelter," Sheriff Islington said. "They're full up, but they might be able to make some kennel space if I explain the situation to them. My only concern is that it wouldn't stop anyone from coming back if they already know or believe the dog is here."

"No, don't do that," Sadie said. Penny gave her a look, but she ignored her. The thought of Cleo in a crowded animal shelter broke her heart. "You're right. Melody and Andrew already know we have her. I think we managed to trick Ford into believing we don't, at least. Why was he looking for her?"

"We're looking into it," Sheriff Islington said. "I want you to be cautious. He has an alibi, but it's not a rock-solid one — an employee at his gym, swears he was there during the time the homicide took place, but the security footage from that evening is conveniently corrupted. We have a pretty good idea of when the shooting happened, since there are a few people in town who heard the gun go off."

"What about Andrew and Melody?" Sadie asked. "Could either of them have killed Damien?"

"I'm not discussing details of the case with the two of you past what I've already said. Just know that we're looking into it. If any of the three come back, call me immediately. For now, just hang in there."

They stood in the doorway and watched him go. Beth's minivan pulled into the parking lot just after he pulled out, and Sadie realized with a jolt that it was time for Rosco to go home already. She would miss the cheerful, young mixed breed being there, but, in a way, it would also be a relief to have him gone. She have one less dog to worry about if something happened with Cleo.

"I don't like this," Penny grumbled as Beth parked the van. "I don't like this at all."

"I know," Sadie said. "But we're stuck for now. Unless you want to send Cleo to the animal shelter."

Penny's shoulders slumped. "No, I don't. She's a sweet girl, and I don't think she would be comfortable there. Still, it sucks."

"We just have to trust that Sheriff Islington will track down the killer before something else happens."

"Yeah, because tiny towns like this are known for having super advanced police departments."

"He managed to catch the motel killer," Sadie muttered. "Smile. We want Beth to keep coming back."

Beth waved as she walked across the parking lot to them, and Sadie waved back, pasting a smile on her face. Penny did the same, then whispered, "I need to finish doing some laundry. You need help with anything?"

"No, I'm good," Sadie whispered back. "Let's figure out what to do for dinner after Rosco leaves."

With a nod, Penny vanished back into the laundry room and Sadie held the door open further so Beth could come in.

"Hi, dear," she said. "Is Rosco ready to go?"

"Just about," Sadie said. "I just need to go pack up his things for you. He was lovely as always, and I'll miss having him here."

She went back into the kennels to fetch Rosco and all of his belongings. All three of the dogs were in the outdoor runs, but he came running in when she called him. She packed his bedding away first, then slipped his collar on and hooked him to his leash. He must have realized Beth was there, because he nearly yanked her arm out of its socket as she led him back through to the lobby. She let the leash go when he saw Beth, and he raced over to her. She bent down and caught him in her arms. Sadie smiled as the two greeted each other.

"There's my handsome boy. Oh, I missed you." Straightening up, she looked at Sadie. "Thanks again for watching him. What do I owe you?"

Sadie checked the file and told Beth what she still owed for this stay. Beth paid the remainder with her card, which always took a second to go through.

While they were waiting for the payment to process, Beth said, "I know you mentioned you were going to do dog training, too. Have you started scheduling classes yet? I'd love to get him in to work on his manners. Once the baby's a little older and he's a little better behaved, I could bring him with me on the weekends instead of leaving him here."

Sadie felt a pang at the thought, Rosco was their only regular customer at the moment, but she knew it would be better for both him and Beth if he could go with her to visit her daughter and grandchild instead of staying here.

"I'm hoping to get that aspect of the business up and running within a month," she said. "I'll make a note to call you as soon as I get things organized. We'll be opening the motel rooms in about a week, and I want to make sure that goes smoothly first."

"I'd appreciate that," Beth said. "I'd love to be your first training clients. And in the meantime, there's no rush. I know you have a lot on your plate. This place looks better every time we come."

"Thanks. We've been hard at work. Do you need help bringing his things out to your car?"

"Oh, if you wouldn't mind. He can be a handful."

Sadie helped Beth pack up her car, then stood in the parking lot and waved as they drove away. When they left, she went back into the lobby, feeling a little bereft. It was just Jasper and Cleo now. They didn't have any other boarding clients lined up until Rosco's stay next weekend. She hoped things would take off soon because, at this rate, they would be closed by Halloween.

"How's the laundry going?" she asked as she stepped into the laundry room. Penny looked up from cleaning a dryer lint screen.

"It's going," she said. "Give me five minutes, then we'll figure out dinner. I know we have all those frozen meals, but I feel like we should celebrate with takeout or something."

"That sounds good to me," Sadie said. "It is a special occasion."

She went through to the kennels. Cleo was still outside, but Jasper was back in and waiting for her at the chain-link door. She reached for the latch but then hesitated, glancing back toward Cleo's kennel. The dog didn't normally spend that much time outside. Frowning, she walked back to the first kennel and opened the door.

"Cleo?" she called out. "Hey, sweetie. Want to come in?"

Nothing. Beginning to worry, she reached for her phone, but it wasn't there. She remembered having it out while she was showing Sheriff Islington the security footage. She must have left it in the lobby.

Feeling the beginning of panic, she hurried to the back of the kennel and knelt down to push the doggie door open so she could peer into the yard outside.

No Cleo.

"Oh, my goodness," she breathed. She backed out of the kennel and raced toward the laundry room door, nearly colliding with Penny as she came through from the other direction.

"Sadie, we need to call—" She broke off. "What happened?"

"Cleo's missing," Sadie said. "Why? What's going on with you?"

"Ford is back. I just saw him come into the lobby. And he looks mad."

CHAPTER TWELVE

Sadie and Penny went out to the lobby together. Ford was waiting at the front desk, but he turned toward them as soon as he heard the laundry room door open.

"There you are. I know you have Cleo, and I know you lied to me last time."

"I'm sorry, sir, I'm going to have to ask you to leave," Sadie said. She approached the front desk, hoping she didn't look as nervous as she felt. "Not only do we not have the dog you're looking for, but even if we did, we couldn't release her to someone who isn't her owner."

"I spoke to Norma Underwood at the hardware store," Ford said. Sadie's stomach sank. "As soon as I showed her Cleo's photo, she told me that the dog was being boarded here. I've known Norma for years, and she's not a liar, which tells me that the two of you are."

Sadie spotted her phone sitting on the counter near Penny's laptop. She needed to check the security footage, but she also needed to deal with Ford. The knowledge that she had somehow lost Cleo made her feel sick to her stomach.

"I'm sorry, but we honestly do not have Cleo," she said as she slipped around to the other side of the desk and picked up her phone,

"Enough with the lies," Ford said. He slapped a paper down on top of the counter.

"What's this?"

"A release form signed by Melody's mother. I'm going to take Cleo to her."

Sadie glanced down at the form, hesitating. She had no way to tell if it was legitimate or not, but it didn't matter — Cleo was missing. She glanced at Penny. Her friend was standing at the back of the lobby, texting frantically on her phone.

"I'm sorry," she said, sliding the paper back across to Ford. "We really don't have her."

"Stop lying," Ford snapped. His face was turning an alarming shade of red, a vein bulging in his temple.

Sadie took a step back and tapped her phone's

screen repeatedly to wake it up. Keeping one eye on him, she quickly navigated to the security camera app and loaded the recent videos from the outdoor camera facing the dog runs.

There it was. Melody walked into view, not even ten minutes ago — she must have been here while Sadie was sending Rosco home — with a pair of bolt cutters. Sadie watched as she cut the padlock on the chain link door to Cleo's run and ushered the dog out before looping a slip lead around her neck and jogging out of sight with her.

"Are you paying attention to me?" Ford snapped. "Listen, I don't know who dropped the dog off, but if it was Melody or her brother, it's imperative that they don't get her back. Not until everything is straightened out."

"I can only release Cleo to her owner," Sadie said. "I'm sorry, but I really can't help you."

"Don't you get it?" Ford asked. "If Melody gets her dog back, she's going to run."

"Run?" Sadie asked. "The last I heard, she was missing after someone was murdered in her home."

"She's going to go on the run with her brother. Andrew is dangerous, and he can convince her to do anything, but she won't leave without Cleo. Look, I have the paper. You can even call Melody's mother to confirm. She agrees with me that Melody shouldn't get Cleo back until this is all straightened out. Give me the dog, and I'll be out of your hair. I'll even pay for her boarding stay myself."

He drew his wallet out of his pocket. Sadie glanced at Penny as her friend slipped into the laundry room, her phone pressed to her ear. She must be calling the police, though who she had texted first, Sadie had no idea.

"I'm sorry," she said firmly. "We can't help you. Melody already picked her up."

Ford froze. He looked at her with something like real fear in his eyes. "When?"

"Five or ten minutes ago," Sadie said. "Listen, you have to leave…"

She couldn't even finish the sentence before he turned around and raced out the door. She followed at a distance, peering outside as he got into his truck, slammed the door shut, and peeled out of the parking lot. Worry clawed up Sadie's throat, and she hurried around to the back of the counter to dig her pepper spray out of her purse. It was a bit late for it, but she felt better having it on her.

She was about to go back into the laundry room to tell Penny that Ford had just left when the lobby door opened again. She spun around with a squeak of surprise, raising the pepper spray, only to find herself pointing it at Sam.

He froze until she lowered the canister.

"I'm sorry," she said. "Melody just stole Cleo, and her ex, Ford, was here looking for her and… what are you doing here?" He reached for his notebook, but she put it together before he started writing. "Oh, Penny texted you, didn't she?"

He nodded. For the first time, she found herself wishing he could talk just so they could communicate faster. She really needed to get on learning sign language.

"What's going on?" Penny asked. Sadie turned to see her poking her head out of the laundry room.

"I told Ford that Melody just took Cleo, and he took off like a bat out of hell," Sadie said.

"Do you think he's going after her?"

"He must be, but I don't know if he could catch up," she said. "They could be a couple miles away by now."

"I mean, he might be able to guess where they're going. They were together for a long time, weren't they?"

"Did you call the sheriff's department?" Sadie asked, her mind racing.

Penny nodded. "They're sending someone out."

"All right… you stay here and deal with all of that. Show them the footage of Melody taking Cleo and tell them what happened." She looked at Sam. "Will you go with me to try to find Ford? I'm worried about what will happen if he finds Melody and Andrew. I saw which direction he turned out of the parking lot — away from town — and there isn't much out that way. If we're lucky, we might be able to catch up."

Sam nodded. She grabbed her purse, slipping her pepper spray and phone inside, and exchanged a quick, worried hug with Penny before following Sam out of the lobby.

CHAPTER THIRTEEN

She and Sam jogged across the parking lot to her SUV. He was still buckling his seatbelt when she pulled out of the parking lot. She turned to the left, away from town, and accelerated as quickly as she dared.

"I'm not sure whether I hope we find them or not," she admitted as they drove. "I still have no idea what's going on. Ford said he thought Melody was at risk of running, but from what? He's her ex, so in a way he's the obvious suspect, but Andrew, her brother, was the one who dropped Cleo off. I talked to Bailey, and she said that, according to Melody, Andrew hated Damien, along with the rest of her friends and family. What if he thought he was protecting his sister by killing him, or found out that

Damien was abusing her or something? He could be the one who shot Damien, then he didn't want to leave Cleo in the apartment, so he took her to be boarded here until he and Melody figured out what they were going to do." She paused, waiting for him to respond, realized he couldn't — she couldn't very well read his notebook while she was driving — then continued, "And then there's Melody herself. Everyone I've spoken to thinks it's strange that she broke up with Ford out of the blue to date someone like Damien. Except, Bailey mentioned Damien just came into some money, so maybe there's something there. Maybe Ford thinks she killed him and now she's going to flee the country with Cleo and Andrew or something."

"What are we going to do if we find them?"

She jumped at the voice and glanced at Sam. He had typed into his phone, and the device had read the words out to her.

"Oh, good idea," she said, refocusing on the road. "I don't know. Make sure Cleo's okay, I guess. I just hate the thought of her being trapped in the middle of something like this. She's the only one I know for a fact is innocent."

Also, Melody had technically stolen Cleo from them; even if she was Cleo's legal owner, she still had to go through the proper checkout process and pay for the dog's stay. Well, Andrew had dropped five-hundred dollars off along with Cleo, but the sheriff still had the money, and asking for payment seemed like a good reason to explain why they had tracked them down.

"What's this way?" she asked. "I'm still not familiar with the area."

"Nothing," the robotic voice from the phone said. And then, *"Florida, if you drive far enough."*

"Geez. We're not going to chase them that far."

They reached a stop sign. She slowed and looked at each of the three directions, trying to figure out which way Ford might have gone. Sam touched her shoulder, then nodded out the window. She saw black tire marks curving to the right and remembered how fast Ford had peeled out of the parking lot.

"Those weren't there yesterday," Sam typed on his phone.

"I guess we're going that way," she said. She hit her blinker and turned. She saw nothing but trees for the next few miles, until the area began to open up a little with a few farmhouses and fields on either side. The next intersection they came to was bigger, with a blinking yellow light and a gas station on the corner.

That was where they got lucky. Andrew's station

wagon and Ford's truck were both there, pulled up along the edge of the parking lot, away from the pumps. She saw Melody standing with Cleo at a distance, while Andrew and Ford faced off. She took the turn into the gas station parking lot fast enough to make her seat belt lock up and pulled to a stop behind the station wagon.

They stepped out of the SUV into the middle of an argument.

"You can't just leave," Ford was saying. Andrew was physically blocking him, but Ford only had eyes for Melody. "We need to talk. Do you really think the police won't track you down if you try to flee?"

"I didn't do anything," Melody said, clinging to Cleo's leash like it was a lifeline. The dog turned toward Sadie, her tail wagging. Melody glanced her way, too. "Who are you? This is private. Please, leave us be."

"I'm the person whose kennel you broke into," Sadie said. "Sadie Barton."

"I... I didn't mean to. I'm sorry about the lock," Melody said. "But please, I can't do this right now. She's my dog, and I knew the police were looking for me, so I couldn't come in through the front to get her. Please, I know my brother left you money. Just let us go."

"It's not Melody the police should be after." Andrew snapped at Ford, ignoring them. "Do you really think we don't both know it was you?"

Ford finally stopped trying to reach Melody. He crossed his arms, looking down at Andrew, whom he towered over. "What are you saying? Say it straight if you're going to accuse me of something."

Andrew, who was definitely the same man who had dropped Cleo off, though he was wearing a different outfit today, didn't look intimidated.

"It's obvious, man," he said. "You couldn't let her go, and everyone knows how much you hated Damien. You said to my face that you would do whatever it took to get her back, and a week later, the man is dead."

"I'm not the only one who hated him," Ford said. "What was it you told me at the bar that night? You thought that loser was going to drag your sister down. You hated him just as much as I did."

"Yeah, Damien was a loser," Andrew said. "But I didn't kill the guy. How do you think it felt to have my sister call me crying when she got home to find a dead body and a terrified dog? We've been sleeping in the car for almost a week, and we had to drop poor Cleo off at some random kennel just to keep her safe. It doesn't matter how I felt about

Damien. I wouldn't do that to my sister, and she knows that."

"Does she?" Ford asked. He turned to look at Melody again. "Do you really believe Andrew wouldn't kill for you, Melody?"

Melody faltered. "I…" She looked between them. "Andrew wouldn't…"

"You told me he beat up one of your exes back in high school, so you already know he's willing to resort to violence, and I know he wasn't shy about telling you how much he hated Damien."

"You hated him, too," Melody said. "And you still had a key to the apartment."

"And Andrew didn't?" Ford took a step closer to her. "I know you don't see it, but you're in danger with him. He's going to keep you isolated from everyone. You're going to spend the rest of your life on the run. Come with me, and I'll keep you safe while this gets sorted out."

He took another step toward her, reaching his hand out. Cleo, the sweet, polite dog Sadie had spent nearly a week caring for, stepped in front of her owner and growled. Melody took a step back.

"She's never done that before," she said, her voice shaking. Her dog's response to Ford seemed to strengthen her resolve. "She's scared of you, Ford. She's never been scared of you before."

"Stupid dog," Ford snapped, glaring down at Cleo. "I should never have gotten her for you."

He turned away. For a second, Sadie relaxed, but then she saw him reach into the waistband of his pants, to withdraw a pistol, which he pointed calmly at Andrew, who froze. His gaze flicked over Sadie and Sam dismissively before he refocused on Melody.

"Drop the leash and get into my truck, or your brother is going to end up the same way Damien did."

"No," Melody whispered. "Please, don't do this."

He settled his finger on the trigger. "You have to the count of three. I'm not playing around. Drop the leash, get into the truck, and buckle your seatbelt. One... two..."

With a sob, Melody dropped Cleo's leash and walked toward Ford's truck, her head bowed. Ford kept his gun trained on Andrew but reached out to place his hand around the back of Melody's neck, guiding her toward the truck as he followed her. Andrew's fists clenched, but he didn't make a move. Sadie couldn't blame him — there was no doubt left now that Ford was the one who killed Damien, so they already knew he was willing to use the gun. One wrong move, and Andrew would be dead.

"Please," Melody said when they reached the truck. "Please don't do this, Ford. Just put the gun down. We can talk…"

"Shut up," he snapped, punctuating the words with a rough shove.

That was his mistake. Cleo, who had taken a few hesitant steps after her owner before glancing back at Sadie, clearly confused by this new turn of events, didn't take kindly toward Ford manhandling Melody. She raced toward him, barking. Ford ignored her and shoved Melody against the truck again, pinning her against it while he reached for the door handle.

That was too much for Cleo, who lunged for his ankle. With a shout, Ford whirled, turning the gun on her, but Melody tackled him, pulling his hand down in the nick of time, so that when the gun went off, the bullet hit the dirt.

Sam and Andrew moved at the same time, both of them rushing Ford, who was quickly overpowering Melody. Sadie hurried forward too, reaching out to grab the end of the slip lead around Cleo's neck. She was worried the dog would turn on her, not out of any malice, but simply redirecting in a stressful situation, but Cleo let herself be pulled out of the fight without struggling. Sam managed to pin Ford's hand against the truck and peeled his fingers away from the gun to throw it to the ground, while Andrew pulled his sister back.

She yanked out of his grasp and ducked to pick up the dropped gun, then aimed it at Ford and Sam. "Get back," she snapped. Sam glanced over her shoulder, saw the gun, and quickly backed away. Ford took a step forward, but Melody put her finger on the trigger.

"Don't think I won't," she said. "I know you don't understand it — neither of you do — but I loved Damien. You killed him. The only thing keeping me from pulling this trigger right now is knowing that if I go to prison, Cleo will miss me. Don't test me, Ford."

Sam retreated to stand by Sadie's side. With a nudge, he slipped her his phone and took Cleo's leash from her. Right, they needed backup, and Sam couldn't talk, and she had left her phone in the SUV with her purse. Dialing 911, she raised the phone to her ear. With a little luck, they had already sent someone out to the motel, and help was only minutes away.

EPILOGUE

"Oh, I can't look," Penny said, covering her eyes and turning away from the screen dramatically. "You do it."

"Coward," Sadie said. She turned the spinning office chair around, forcing Penny to face the screen. "We're doing this together."

Penny took a deep breath and peeled her fingers away from her eyes, one by one, to squint at the screen. "All right, open it."

Sadie clicked the email from the state inspection office. She read the first few lines and breathed out a sigh in a rush of relief. "We did it. We passed the inspection. We can open the motel."

Penny squealed and hugged her so tightly, Sadie was worried her ribs might crack. Jasper, excited by the commotion, danced around them, his whip-like tail whacking Sadie in the back of the thighs. She laughed and pulled away from Penny to bend down and thump the dog's sides.

"That's right, Jasper. We did it. We're going to have lots of guests every single day from here on out."

"This calls for more celebration," Penny said. "I'll go get the other bottle of champagne."

While Penny went to fetch the bubbly drink, Sadie took over the office chair. She flopped down on the seat and let her momentum roll it across the floor. She realized that for the first time since they bought the place, she didn't have a feeling of dread sitting on her chest. There was no guarantee they would get enough business to stay open, especially with the reputation the motel had, but they had done everything they could, and all that was left was to wait and see if their hard work would pay off.

Cleo's situation having been resolved was another relief. She called Jasper over and smoothed her hands over his velvety soft ears. Melody had stopped by a couple of days ago to apologize for breaking Cleo out and to hand over a new padlock. Sadie had already replaced the one she cut through, but she thanked her anyway and spent some time chatting with her. She learned Melody and Cleo were going to be staying with her brother until she could find a new place to live. She said there was no way she was going back to her apartment, and Sadie didn't blame her. She felt the same way about Room Ten, though she didn't have the option of picking up and moving somewhere else as easily as Melody did.

She hoped she would see Cleo again, but mostly she was just glad that things had turned out all right for the dog and her owner. Her own breakup still stung, but the discovery that her boyfriend was covering for his best friend while he cheated on Penny was nowhere near as bad as Melody's experience with her ex had been. It put things into perspective for her, just a little. Things could always be worse.

The lobby door opened, and Penny came back inside, a bottle of champagne and two flutes in her hands.

"We should have a party," she said. "You can text Sam. I'll see if Bailey wants to come; I bet she'll bring cookies if she does. This is it, Sadie. This is the beginning of everything."

She poured the champagne, and they raised their glasses in a toast to the start of something good.

Printed in Dunstable, United Kingdom